Penguin Cha-Cha

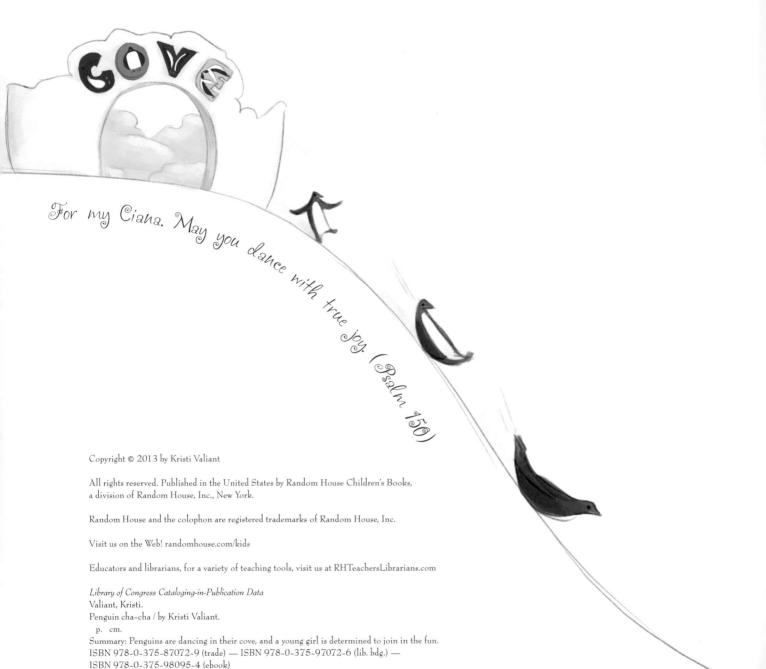

For my Ciana. May you dance with true joy. (Psalm 150)

Library of Congress Cataloging-in-Publication Data
Valiant, Kristi.
Penguin cha-cha / by Kristi Valiant.
   p. cm.
Summary: Penguins are dancing in their cove, and a young girl is determined to join in the fun.
ISBN 978-0-375-87072-9 (trade) — ISBN 978-0-375-97072-6 (lib. bdg.) —
ISBN 978-0-375-98095-4 (ebook)
[1. Penguins—Fiction. 2. Dance—Fiction.] I. Title.
PZ7.V2537Pe 2013   [E]—dc23 2012016265

MANUFACTURED IN MALAYSIA

10 9 8 7 6 5 4 3 2 1
First Edition

Penguin Cha-Cha

Kristi Valiant

TODAY: Dancing

BACKSTAGE

Random House 🏠 New York

Julia was wild about everything at the Romping Chomping Park and Zoo, especially the shows. Every weekend, she shimmied up a tall tree and watched the performance.

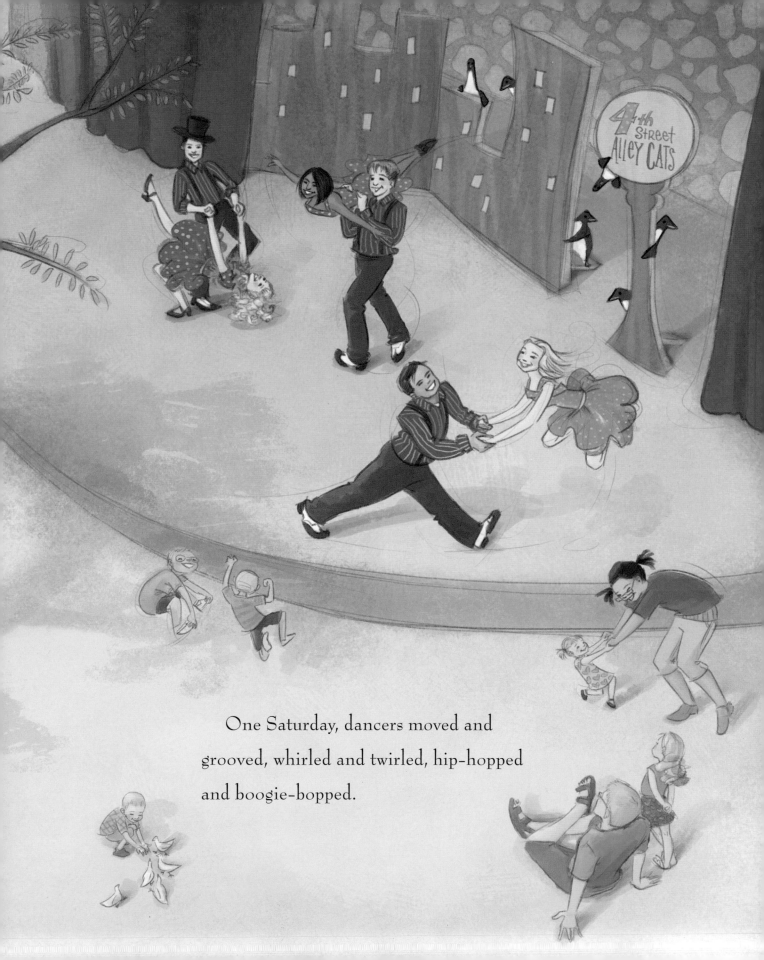

One Saturday, dancers moved and
grooved, whirled and twirled, hip-hopped
and boogie-bopped.

When a dancer tossed her feather boa backstage, Julia noticed a sneaky flipper snatch it in midair. Penguins pounced on hats and clothes, fans and bows.

Just what are those fishy penguins up to? Julia wondered.

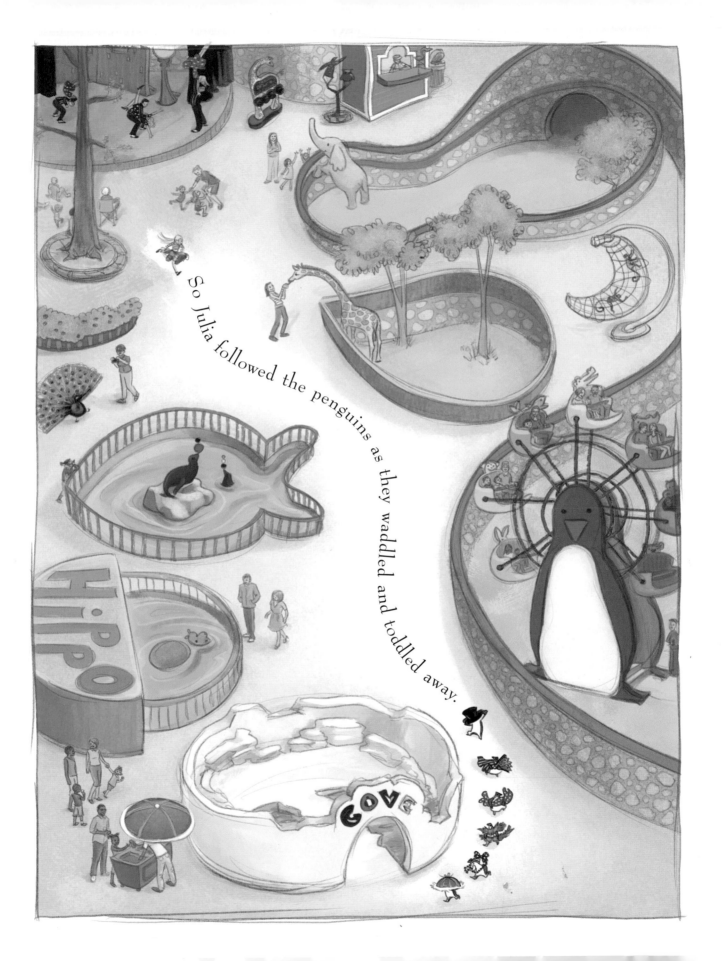

So Julia followed the penguins as they waddled and toddled away.

When she got to the Penguin Cove,
she peeked inside. The penguins stared
back at her. Julia saw no hats. No clothes.
No fans. No bows.

Just what are those fishy penguins up to?
Julia wondered.

So Julia spied on the penguins from way up high. Were they moving and grooving? Whirling and twirling? Hip-hopping and boogie-bopping? Yes! The penguins were dancing!

She couldn't believe it! She
had to tell someone.

"Dancing penguins, you say?
Nonsense!" said the zookeeper.
"Penguins can't hip and hop and
boogie and bop. Why don't you
go and take another look-see."

Julia grabbed a
top hat and ran to join
the jazzy jitterbug.

She bounded into the Penguin Cove and shouted,
"Let's dance!"

The penguins didn't flap a flipper.

They didn't shake a tail feather.

They froze like penguin Popsicles.

But when no one was around,
the penguins were having a toe-tapping,
knee-knocking, rocking good time.

and wove all over the cove!

Still, the penguins didn't budge.

Julia trudged home.

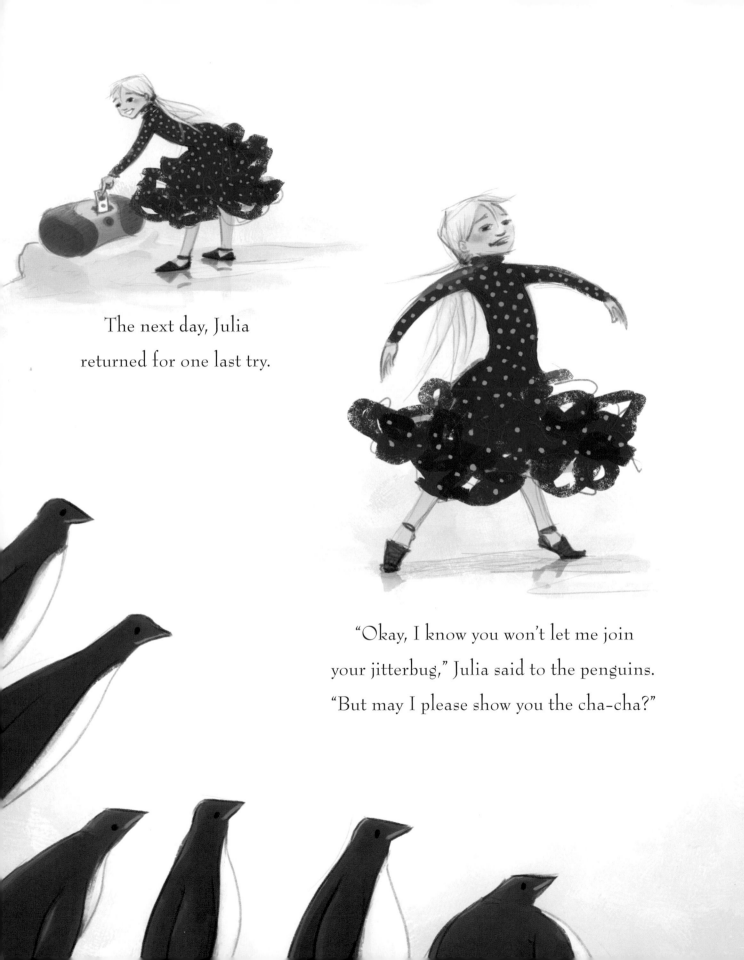

The next day, Julia
returned for one last try.

"Okay, I know you won't let me join
your jitterbug," Julia said to the penguins.
"But may I please show you the cha-cha?"

Step,
step,
cha-cha-cha.

Step,
step,
cha-cha-cha.

Julia clapped, cha-cha-cha.
Julia snapped, cha-cha-cha.
Julia spun, cha-cha-cha.
Julia swung, cha-cha-cha.

And suddenly she heard . . .

Tap,
flap,
cha-cha-cha.

Tap,
flap,
cha-cha-cha.

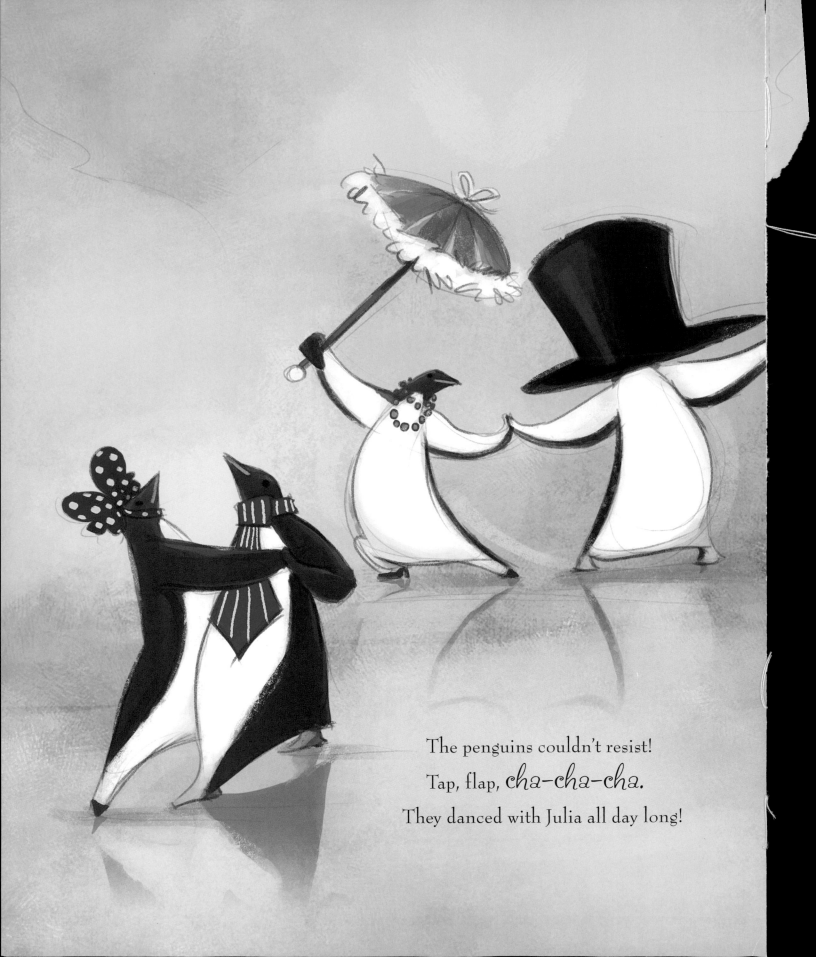

The penguins couldn't resist!
Tap, flap, cha-cha-cha.
They danced with Julia all day long!

From then on, Julia always kept
her penguin costume handy.

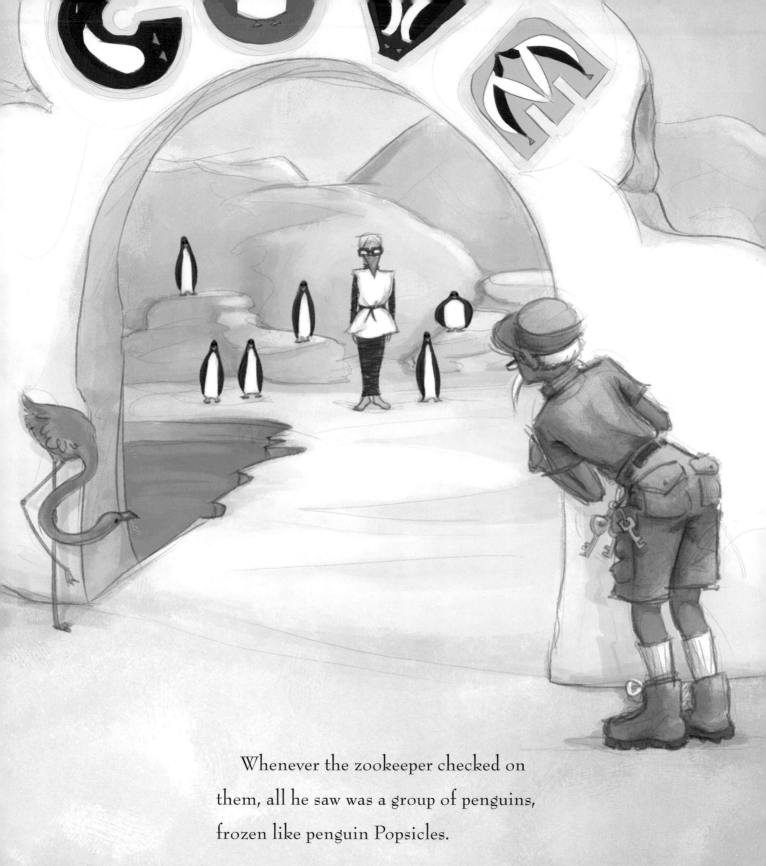

Whenever the zookeeper checked on them, all he saw was a group of penguins, frozen like penguin Popsicles.

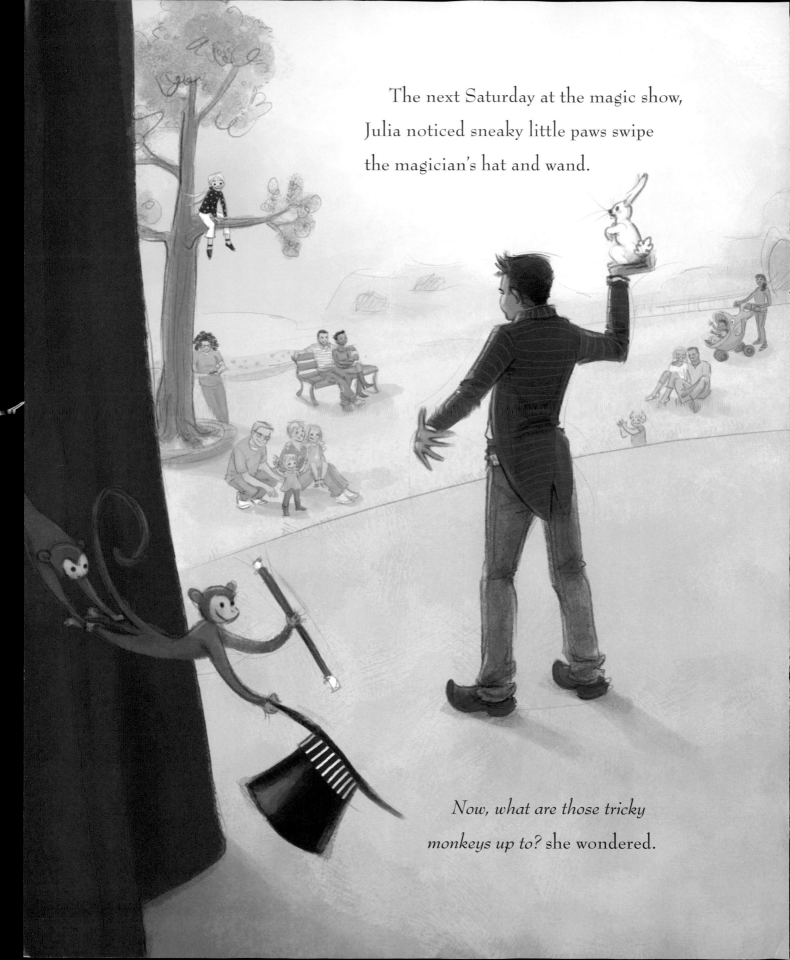

The next Saturday at the magic show,
Julia noticed sneaky little paws swipe
the magician's hat and wand.

*Now, what are those tricky
monkeys up to?* she wondered.